TBH, I Feel the Same

Also by Lisa Greenwald

The Friendship List Series
11 Before 12
12 Before 13
13 and Counting

The TBH Series
TBH, This Is SO Awkward
TBH, This May Be TMI
TBH, Too Much Drama
TBH, IDK What's Next

TBH, I Feel the Same

KATHERINE TEGEN BOOKS
An Imprint of HarperCollins Publishers

BY LISA GREENWALD
Author of the Friendship List series

Katherine Tegen Books is an imprint of HarperCollins Publishers.

TBH #5: TBH, I Feel the Same

www.harpercollinschildrens.com

ISBN 978-0-06-290622-9

Typography by Molly Fehr
19 20 21 22 23 SCP 10 9 8 7 6 5 4 3 2 1
❖
First Edition

For my friends who went to
Outdoor Ed with me in 1993:
Blair, Lynne, Randi, Sarah, and Sonia

From: Victoria Melford
To: Gabrielle Katz, Prianka Basak, Cecily Anderson
FWD: Subject: Fall Trip!

Hiiiiii loovieeeesss!!!

So excited 4 swim! Don't forget bathing suits! Plus WOO WOOOOOOOO about this trip & 7th grade. Can't wait MY LOVIES! SOOOOO excited.

Love you all!!!!!
Victoria Melford the Fabulous!

> **From:** Yorkville Middle School Administration
> **To:** Yorkville seventh-grade students and parents
> **Subject:** Fall Trip!
>
> Dear families:
>
> Welcome back to another fabulous Yorkville year! We hope you all enjoyed your summers.

As you may know, in late September, the entire seventh grade embarks on an Outdoor Education trip to a nature center in upstate New York.

You'll be receiving materials about the trip in the mail, but please come to the information session on Friday morning, right after drop-off.

See you there.

Edward Carransey
Principal

You must be the change you want to see in the world.
—Gandhi

1st day of 7th gradeeeeeeee

PRIANKA

Omg I know this is rude to do but what is Sami even saying rn 🙎🏻‍♀️🤨

She has literally never talked to us b4 in her whole life 🤣 🤣

CECILY

Hahah

I think she feels awk in the courtyard w/o her friends 😬 😝 🤣

PRIANKA

Gabs is so busy talking 2 her she isn't feeling her vibrations 📱➡️📱📱

CECILY

LOL

CECILY

Kind of awk to text about her tho rn while she is talking 2 us 🫥

PRIANKA

Where is Vic

CECILY

IDK

Late on 1st day???

PRIANKA

Hmmmmm

Can't believe Gabs still hasn't looked @ her fone

CECILY

Ok let's stop texting 4 real now

Guysssss why is the phone policy even stricter this year? It's the first day and we've barely had time to talk between classes and now we can't even text in the hallway. Hopefully you check lockers before lunch. Let's sit at the back table on the right. It's the best spot because it's near the salad bar.

PS I snuck to photocopy this in the library to give to all of you. LOL.
Love, Gabs

So sorry! Just saw this and now I'm on the bus with u guys and obv we found each other but I still wanted to write back. Sooooooo happy we all got to eat lunch together. Thrilled I got the grade's lunch schedules changed. I like our new table. And yay we all survived the first day. Xoxoxox Cece

SWIM TEAM WOO HOO

PRIANKA

Guysssss I had to run home & get my bathing suit for swim team

Forgot to pack it

See u guys there

CECILY

Pri, where r u ???

We r about 2 go in the pool

Hi Cecily,
I want to talk to you sort of face-to-face but sort of not. Can you meet me on the little strip of sidewalk between our houses after we get home from swim team?
Love, Mara

Yes. Sorry this note is wet with pool water. Why didn't you just text me? Xo Cece

I forgot my phone! :(

UMMMMMM

CECILY

Um guys that swim practice was insane

How r we going 2 do that 3x a week

GABRIELLE

No clue

I don't even feel like doing it anymore

PRIANKA

Same

Can we bail

VICTORIA

Guysssssss

VICTORIA

We made a commitment

It only goes thru December

CECILY

Ugggghhhh IDK

& I heard they r posting info about play tryouts soon

I wanna do that 2

I'm gonna be sooooooo busy

PRIANKA

I just wanna hang out & watch tv 📺 📺

Is that bad 🤔 🤔 🤔 🤔 🤔

GABRIELLE

LOL Pri 😆 🤣 😆

VICTORIA

Guys come on 😳 😳

9

VICTORIA

We were so excited about it

GABRIELLE

IK but that's bc it was summer

Now I'm in fall mode

I just wanna wear sweaters and eat cider
donuts

PRIANKA

LOL

Now Gabs is speaking my language

CECILY

LOL LOL 🤣😂🤣😂🤣😂

VICTORIA

Whatevs peeps 😾😼😾

Talk laterzzzzz

Mara, Cecily

MARA

I know it's awk that I am texting u & we r
standing next 2 each other

CECILY

Yeah what's up

MARA

I wanted 2 talk 2 u but it's hard 2 actually
talk

Know what I mean

CECILY

Kinda yeah

MARA

I feel like I just want 2 be friends & not anything more but I don't want it to be weird

CECILY

TBH I was feeling the same way

MARA

Really?

CECILY

Ya I feel like 7th grade is super busy & stuff & I just don't want any awkwardness

MARA

Agree

CECILY

We r still BNF tho

MARA

BNF?

CECILY

Best neighbors forever duh

MARA

Oh LOL yes

CECILY

K gonna say gnight IRL now

FYI

CECILY

Guys fyi Mara & I r just friends now

PRIANKA

  R u ok

CECILY

Yeah I am so relieved

I was feeling this way and so was she
✓ ✓ ✓

GABRIELLE

Oh cool 😎 😎

VICTORIA

Glad u r ok 🥰 🥰

Now u need a new crush 🤔 🤔

CECILY

Nooooo just wanna do my own thing now 🙅 🙅

VICTORIA

LOL ok 😂

PRIANKA

Not everyone is like u & Arj, Vic 💑 💑

VICTORIA

Haha

CECILY

K going 2 sleep 4 real 😴 😴 😴

Same

PRIANKA

Love u guysssss 🤍 🤍 🤍

VICTORIA

Ditto 4ever 💞 💞 💞

ATTENTION, YORKVILLE STUDENTS!

Come try out for the Yorkville Middle School musical! Information sessions will take place during all lunch periods TODAY. Grab your food and meet in the auditorium.

See you there!

Ms. Golota & the theater department staff

Home sick

V G C P

VICTORIA

Guyssssss I don't know if u will c this but
I'm home sick today

Fever wahhhh 😦 😦 😦

Hope u don't get it

Do germs spread quickly in a pool???
 🫢

17

Leaving you all locker notes to tell you I won't be at lunch. Going to the play info session! So don't wait for me to sit. Pulled a Gabs and photocopied this in the library. LOL. Xoxoxo Cece

Guysssssss—passing this to Gabs and then pls
pass along—I need to speak to my guidance
counselor about switching electives. I am not
into astronomy. I just realized there's a poetry
elective! How me is that?! Anyway, won't be
@ lunch. Sorry to miss u all! Smooches, Pri
PS Write back! This notebook is lonely!

OMG no one is going to be @ lunch???? What am I
going to do? I am crying for real. :(Luv, Gabs
PS I miss this notebook. Glad it's back in action!
PPS But will any of you even see this?????

Lunchieeeessssss

SAMI

Gabs! So glad u sat w/ us @ lunch

Did you ever find out where ur friends were?

GABRIELLE

All diff stuff 🤔 🤔

Will explain later

I had fun @ ur table btw

MIRIAM

Sit w/ us again!!!!!!!! 🙌 🙌 🤞

GABRIELLE

LOL ok 👍 👍

ELOISE

Did u just come to this school 🏫 🏫 🏫

Why did we not know u last yr ❓❓

GABRIELLE

IDK I was here 😊

ELOISE

Ha ok 😊 🤣

HANNAH P

Gabby remember when we were in that dance class in preschool 🐨 🐨

GABRIELLE

LOL yeah 😊 🤣

I had an accident in my tutu 😳 😳 😳

& I had to wear a random leotard from lost & found and it was soooooooo big on me 😰 😰 😰

21

HANNAH P

Omg I vaguely remember that

SAMI

For reallllls Gabssss

SAMI

Ur so funny

Can't wait to tell u guys about my super secret project

Will be ready to reveal tomorrow I think

GABRIELLE

MIRIAM

K c u guys laterrsssss

HANNAH P

Peace

HANNAH F

Tata

22

SAMI

Xoxo

GABRIELLE

Bye!

OMG LUNCH

G V P C

GABRIELLE

U guys I was the only one out of all of us @ lunch

VICTORIA

Omg 4 real? 😲

GABRIELLE

Yes! 😾 😾

Cece was @ play info session, Pri @ guidance, Vic home sick (sorry for rhyme LOL)

PRIANKA

So where did u sit

So sorry, Gabs!! 🙀🙀🙀

GABRIELLE

Ur never gonna believe this

CECILY

???

GABRIELLE

I sat with the middle table

PRIANKA

Front row middle? 😦😦😦

VICTORIA

OMG 🙃🙃🙃

GABRIELLE

IK

CECILY

U sat with Sami and them ⁉️‼️⁉️‼️‼️

GABRIELLE

Yeah I was talking to Miriam a little in science ♻️ 🗑️ ♻️ ⚛️ ⚛️ ⚛️

So when I was walking by, she was like come sit w/ us 🌭 🍔 🍕 △ △ 🍳 🥗 ⭕ 🍜

PRIANKA

That is insane 😧 😧 😧 😧 😧

GABRIELLE

IK 😬 😬

CECILY

No one new ever sits w/ them 🚫 🚫 🚫 🚫 🚫 🚫

GABRIELLE

IK 😬 😬 😬 😬 😬 😬 😬 😬

VICTORIA

You sat with the Hannahs, too ❓ ❓ ❓

GABRIELLE

Just Hannah P

25

I think Hannah F was @ the play info session

CECILY

Ya she was ✅ ✅

VICTORIA

This is so crazy ‼️‼️‼️‼️

GABRIELLE

Calm down guys it's ok

PRIANKA

Ok I need 2 finish this poetry thing since I'm switching in tomorrow

We were told to write a poem out of random words but all I have is this list so far

Earth
Love
Peace
Humanity
Helpers

PRIANKA

Sunshine
Rest
Artichokes

LOL

CECILY

Oh yay

I need 2 finish math

Will tell u all about the play on the bus

PRIANKA

K

GABRIELLE

Kk

VICTORIA

Mwah 😘 😘 😘

27

Prianka Basak
Poetry Elective

I have found my voice
It sounds like this
Frustration
Exhaustion
Contentment
Happiness
Laughter
I have found my voice
But it's always changing
Sometimes low
Sometimes high-pitched
Sometimes a whisper
I have found my voice
And I demand to be heard

Prianka, Cecily

PRIANKA

K I know we said we were going 2 bed

But is Gabs gonna sit @ the middle table now

Like from now on

Not 2 side chat but just curious...

CECILY

IDK

PRIANKA

She didn't say

CECILY

IK

PRIANKA

Hmmmm

PRIANKA

R u there

CECILY

Y

PRIANKA

K I can tell ur busy

C u tomrw

CECILY

Xox

Tryouts for the musical will be
Monday after school.

See you there!
Ms. Golota & the theater
department staff

Gabrielle, Prianka, Cecily, Victoria

GABRIELLE

Guys my mom is driving me 2day since we have the meeting about the fall trip

PRIANKA

Same

CECILY

Same ✅✅

VICTORIA

Same ✅✅✅

Hahahahah this cracks me up 😂 🤸 😂

CECILY

Me 2 😂 😂 😂 😂

Do u guys want 2 sleep over this weekend & do crafts

VICTORIA

I was thinking ice skating

GABRIELLE

IDK my plans yet

CECILY

For real, Gabs?

Ur always with us

GABRIELLE

IDK don't freak

PRIANKA

I'm away one day this weekend visiting
Dad's college friend 👧👧

But I could be into crafts
🎨🎨🎨🎨🎨🎨

Maybe decorating my new poetry journal

CECILY

Doesn't a whole craft day sound so fun tho
?

VICTORIA

I'm in 🎉 🎉 🎉 ✨ 👯 ✨

GABRIELLE

Pos

Ttyl

OMG we have random bunks!!!!

I know. :(

It won't be that bad. It's only 2 nights.

Wahhhhh. Why can't we pick bunkmates?

They just answered that! So we can branch out.
LOL

What if we are stuck with people who have
super bad BO?

Stop. But ew.

Guys our moms totally know we are passing notes

Sage, Prianka

SAGE

So fun to be ur partner in poetry today

PRIANKA

IK ur so talented

SAGE

Ha not really but thx

PRIANKA

Do we do the peer review thing again tomorrow

SAGE

🙇🙇 I think so

PRIANKA

K cool

SAGE

R u excited for the outdoor ed thing

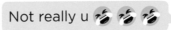
PRIANKA

Not really u

SAGE

Yesssssss I love nature

PRIANKA

LOL I went on a camping thing over
the summer and haaaaated it
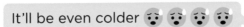

SAGE

Maybe this one will be diff 🤧 🤧

PRIANKA

Maybe but IDK 🤨 🤨 🤨 🤨 🤨 🤨

It'll be even colder 🥶 🥶 🥶 🥶

I am an indoor gal 🏘 🏘 🏘

SAGE

LOL ur funny 😂 😂

PRIANKA

Poetry is...
freedom
emotion
putting yourself out there
feeling your feelings
knowing yourself
connection
calm
peace

From: Gabrielle Katz
To: Ivy Garstein
Subject: hiiiiiiiii

Ivy!!!

I miss you! How's school so far? The craziest thing happened. None of my friends were at lunch because of different things and I ended up sitting at the popular table. Does your school have one? You probably sit at it. LOL. Anyway, I'm not super popular but I'm not unpopular. I'm just regular. But I talked to one of the girls during science and then I sat with them and it was no big deal. It was kind of fun. But now where do I sit? With my friends or them? We can't really combine tables because we wouldn't all fit. Yesterday I skipped lunch to go to some volunteer community service thing but mostly I was stressed about where to sit. UGH. Okay, write back and help meeeeeee!!!!

Love you,
Gabs

From: Sally B. Wembly
To: Yorkville Swim Team
Subject: First meet!

Hi, swimmers!

Just a reminder that our first meet is a week from Saturday! Please meet at the Westville Creek Pool at 8 a.m., ready to swim! Feel free to invite family and friends.

Here's your Sally B. Wembly approved inspirational quote of the day: "It is never too late to be what you might have been." —George Eliot

Anyone want to guess my middle name? :)

See you there!
Coach Sally B. Wembly

From: Ivy Garstein
To: Gabrielle Katz
Subject: RE: hiiiiiiiii

Gabs!

OMG. I know what you're going through. Lunch table drama is the real deal. For some reason my school has assigned lunch tables. Maybe because it's a private school? IDK. Anyway I feel your pain. My cousin Izzy is always whining to me about this.

For some reason, I totally thought you were one of the popular people at school. LOL. Everyone at camp LOVED you!!!!! So anyway, you are popular to me.

Was it always this way with those girls? Has it been like a set table for life?

Xoxo Ivy

JOSEPH AND THE AMAZING TECHNICOLOR DREAMCOAT

NARRATOR
The directors have decided to cast one or many narrators

JOSEPH

JACOB

PHARAOH

BROTHERS
Reuben, Simeon, Levi, Naphtali, Issachar, Asher,
Dan, Zebulun, Gad, Benjamin, Judah

POTIPHAR

MRS. POTIPHAR
Potiphar's wife

BUTLER

BAKER

ENSEMBLE
We are hoping to find 15–20 talented actors and singers to play
wives, servants, Ishmaelites, Elvis dancers, and oh so much more!

See you at auditions!

DRAMA FOR REAL :)

CECILY

Omggggg I am so nervous for auditions 🎭🎭

IDEK what part I want ackkkkkkkkkkk

Did u see the cast list posted by the music room 🎵🎶🎵🎼🎹

Hellooooo where r u peeps ❓❓❓

I feel like I haven't seen u in dayssssss 😔😟😔😩

Can we plleeeeeaaaaseeeee all be @ lunch tomw 🙇🙇🙇

VICTORIA

Hiiiii 👋

Sorry was catching up on hw 😼😼

VICTORIA

VICTORIA

finally feeling better

CECILY

Yayyyyyyyy

From: Gabrielle Katz
To: Ivy Garstein
Subject: RE: hiiiiiiiii

Hi Ivy,

Um, no. It wasn't like this at all before like the very end of last year. I think everyone was just adjusting to middle school in 6th grade and we go to a huge school so, like, no one even knew who was popular and stuff. There was one crew called the M-girls that people thought were sooooo awesome but they have kind of disbanded. Anyway, at the end of last year, in like June, this group of girls became like a solid thing and they sat at this one table in the cafeteria and then it was like known that they were popular. They're not mean really. I don't know them so well. But they seem nice. I'm not sure. I kind of want to sit with them again. But I don't want to hurt my friends' feelings. I feel like it would be good to branch out, though. What should I do???

I am stressed!

Xoxo Gabs

Ingrid, Cecily

INGRID

Cecily, my darling sister

Please stop singing

INGRID

It is 11 pm

I must sleep

CECILY

Auditions are so soon

Leave me alone

INGRID

Practice must cease by 10 pm

ENOUGH

CECILY

Ur mean

INGRID

Good night

Sami, Hannah P., Hannah F., Miriam, Eloise, Gabby

SAMI

So what do you guys think of my idea ????

In a way it's kind of something 2 get 2 know more girls in the grade 😶 😶

Where r u guyssss 😕 😕 😕 😕

From: Yorkville Middle School Administration
To: Yorkville seventh-grade students and parents
Subject: Outdoor Ed

Dear all:

It was delightful to see everyone at the information session. I know we're all getting excited about this special opportunity. In the coming weeks you'll be receiving more information, including packing lists and a code-of-conduct sheet that must be signed by student and guardian.

Each student will receive a journal in their English classes. They'll write expectations and goals for the trip and they'll continue journaling while at Camp Greensong. Please feel free to reach out to me with any questions or concerns.

All my very best,
Edward Carransey
Principal

You must be the change you want to see in the world.
—Gandhi

Guys, I'm skipping lunch again. Need to talk to Mr. Latigno in the resource center about math. SO lost. ALREADY. Help. Love, Gabs

Just bring your math stuff to lunch and I'll help! We haven't seen you @ lunch in days. What's going on? HERE TO HELP! Xox Cecily

Gabs, for real. Come to lunch. We miss you!!!!! The only time I can talk to you is when we're both in bathing suits. LOL. Smooches, Pri

Ditto. I'll share my curry chicken salad wrap with you. SO GOOD. Pleaaaaasssseeeee. Love, Vic

Miriam, Gabrielle

M   G

MIRIAM

Gabs where were u @ lunch 🥟🥟🥐🥗🥣

We saved u a 🪑

GABRIELLE

Oh um math extra help ✖➕➖➗ 1️⃣2️⃣3️⃣4️⃣5️⃣6️⃣7️⃣8️⃣9️⃣🔟

MIRIAM

I can help u 🆘🆘

I love math 👩👩👩

GABRIELLE

Oh cool 👐👐

MIRIAM

Sit w/ us tomorrow 👌🙏✌🥗🥄

K l gg

MIRIAM

Peace

LUNCH UPDATES

GABRIELLE

Anyone there

Need 2 talk 2 all of u

CECILY

Hiiiiiii practicing my audition stuff

PRIANKA

Writing poetry LOL

51

VICTORIA

Discovered this old show Full House

PRIANKA

Love that show 🤍

GABRIELLE

Anyway...

I'm having some lunch drama

I think u know what I mean...

I want 2 propose a plan

I alternate where I sit @ lunch

One day w/ u guys ✗✗

One day at the middle table 🍽🍽

Hello

GABRIELLE

Anyone there ⁉️❓❓⁉️

VICTORIA

Hi I'm here

CECILY

That is kind of crazy, Gabs, no offense
😵 😵

PRIANKA

Seriously 🙄 🙄 🙄

Especially after Cecily fought for us all 2 have lunch 2gether and not be divided up w/ honors and stuff 😒 😟 😕 🤔 🤦‍♀️

GABRIELLE

IK 🙁

I luv u guys & that's why I'll sit w/ u every other day ☮️ ✌️ 💐

But I had fun with Sami and Miriam and them, too 🙄 🙄 🙄

53

VICTORIA

Could we combine tables

GABRIELLE

I thought about that but we wouldn't fit

I just feel like I kinda wanna hang w/ other people 2

VICTORIA

I am sad

PRIANKA

Same

CECILY

Obv u can do whatever u want 2 do, Gabs

GABRIELLE

Ok

PRIANKA

I gg love ya

CECILY

Xoxo

VICTORIA

Mwah

GABRIELLE

Mwah

What is Gabby thinking?
Switching lunch tables every other day?
It doesn't make sense
I am so angry
You can't depend on anyone anymore
Nothing is forever
This isn't even poetry
I am just so mad

From: Cecily Anderson
To: Prianka Basak, Victoria Melford
Subject: NO SIDE CHATS

Hi guys,

I know we're all upset about Gabby and lunch. First of all, no side chats. I want to remind you. This doesn't count because it's an email and also because we are concerned about her and not being gossipy or mean.

That brings me to my next point. I think we need to be supportive. If we get angry it will only make her want to leave forever. Do you see what I'm saying? Also, I'm very stressed with play auditions and can't handle any more drama. LOL. You know what I mean. So please, let's stay calm.

Love, Cecily

I am not afraid of storms, for I am learning how to sail my ship. —Louisa May Alcott

Colin, Gabrielle

COLIN

Hi

GABRIELLE

Hi

COLIN

I never see u anymore

Can't believe we don't have any classes together

GABRIELLE

IK

COLIN

So whatsup

GABRIELLE

IDK busy

COLIN

Oh

GABRIELLE

See you around

COLIN

See ya

From: Ivy Garstein
To: Gabrielle Katz
Subject: What's up????

Dear Gabs,

So what's going on? You never updated me on the lunch thing. Also, you never told me anything about Colin. Do you still like him?

When can you come visit me? I really miss you. Are you doing the camping trip again? I hope so. I am signing up for the 6 week one this summer. Would you want to do that with me?

So many questions. :)

Lots of love, Ivy

Sami, Hannah P, Hannah F, Gabrielle, Eloise, Miriam

SAMI

Hi guyssss

FYI I am officially over emojis

Not doing it anymore

Too babyish

Anywayyyyyyyyy, soooooo glad you're on board with this ranking thing

I think it'll be fun & remember it's JUST FOR US

Don't tell anyone!

I'll do the categories & then u guys can fill in people since some of us know more people than others do

SAMI

Okay ur prob all asleep

Just realized it's after 10 pm

Oooops

Lucky me I get to keep my phone in my
roooooommmmmmm

K bye

YORKVILLE SWIM TEAM KEY INFORMATION:

Who We Swim Against This Season:

**Fieldston Lake, Barnham Hill,
Waverly Heights, and Clover Creek**

Event Order:

200 Medley Relay	100 Free	100 IM	50 Free //	50 Butterfly
200 Free	200 Free Relay //	50 Back	50 Breast	400 Free Relay

Meet Schedule:

Date	Location	Warm-up Time
Saturday, Nov. 7	Yorkville Aquatic Center	5:00 p.m.
Saturday, Nov. 14	Fieldston Lake Aquatic Center	5:30 p.m.
Saturday, Dec. 5 *(We Host)	Barnham Hill Aquatic Center	5:30 p.m.
Saturday, Dec. 12	Waverly Heights Aquatic Center	7:00 p.m.
Saturday, Dec. 19	Clover Creek Aquatic Center	5:30 p.m.

PHEWWWWW

VICTORIA

Soooooo happy we don't have a meet until November

Was not ready

GABRIELLE

OMG same

PRIANKA

I am feeling it more now

CECILY

I need 2 drop out I think 😨😨😨😨😨

Too busy w/ the play 🎭😹🎭😹

VICTORIA

We were supposed 2 do this 2gether 😾😾

😾😾😾

PRIANKA

I'm still in, Vic 🏞️ 🏞️ 🏞️

VICTORIA

K

but guysssssss

I really want to hang as much as we can!!
👍 👍 👍 👧👧👧 👩 👩

CECILY

we will, for real

please don't stress

but we all have diff interests & want to do all kinds of stuff

VICTORIA

I know I know

GABRIELLE

k no more drama

love u allllllllll

From: Gabrielle Katz
To: Ivy Garstein
Subject: Hi

Hi, Ivy:

Sorry I haven't updated you. First of all, I don't think I like Colin. I barely see him. I don't think I like anyone. I have too much friend drama for boys. I told Cece, Pri, and Victoria that I'd alternate tables but they were kind of annoyed by it, so I decided not to do it. But they still seem annoyed. I don't know. We are going on this Outdoor Ed trip with my grade soon. I wonder if it will be like our camping trip. I hope so!

We need to plan a sleepover.

Isn't it crazy how no one ever posts in the camp online album anymore? Everyone is over it, I guess.

Love, Gabs

Hi, Sage—here's my newest poem. Let me know what you think. Thanks! Prianka

What Fall Smells Like

Like wet leaves
Dampness
And rain
Like fireplaces off in the distance
Smokiness
And pajamas fresh from the dryer
Like apple cider
Coziness
And knee socks
Like deep breaths
Warmth
Togetherness

Hi, Prianka. Here's mine. I'm not sure I'm really talking about smell here. But who knows... xoxo Sage

What Fall Smells Like

Crisp
Cold
But then sometimes hot
Sticky
Ices melting on the concrete
But then cool again
Wool sweaters
Plastic packages of tights being ripped open
Sticky fingers from cider donuts
Apple orchards with most of the apples
On the grass
Hayrides
And pumpkin guts
And candy corn
Fall smells like food
And traditions
And change

From: Ivy Garstein
To: Gabrielle Katz
Subject: RE: Hi

Hey, Gabs,

Sorry about all the drama. It's hard to change friend groups. I feel like you need to remember how awesome you are, though, and how everyone loves you and that's why you're even in this position in the first place! You branched out at camp and now you know you can do it at school, too!!!! Everyone wants to be friends with you!!!!

Sorry about Colin. I don't like anyone either now. Everyone else does, though. Whatever.

The Outdoor Ed thing sounds cool. I wish my school did a trip like that. We do a big 8th grade trip somewhere. I think Washington, DC. So there's that at least.

Love, Ivy

OMG

GABRIELLE

Guys those girls are sooooo good @

Where do they go to school

CECILY

They go to the Catholic school near the library 📚 📚 📚 📚

VICTORIA

Oh Sacred Heart 🏫 🏫 🏫

PRIANKA

Yeah

They wear uniforms every day

GABRIELLE

Whoa

They r 4 real the best swimmers

PRIANKA

IK

R u guys freezing rn

GABRIELLE

I am

PRIANKA

I think I may bring a robe next time

VICTORIA

Same

TBH, Gabs, I am so glad u r @ our table 4 lunch

& ur not doing the switching back & forth thing

VICTORIA

I haven't said anything but I need 2 tell u how happy I am 😊 🤍 😬 😁

GABRIELLE

Aw thanx 😊 😊

CECILY

Me 2 😊 😊 😊 😊 😊 😊 😊

PRIANKA

Do Miriam & Sami and the Hannahs miss u?

GABRIELLE

IDK I see them in class

Miriam is my notes buddy 4 history

CECILY

What is a notes buddy

GABRIELLE

We share notes b4 tests

CECILY

Oh

GABRIELLE

Guess u don't have that in honors LOL

CECILY

Grrrrr

PRIANKA

Who decided they r popular peeps anyway

We never had popular b4

GABRIELLE

IDK

This feels awk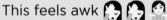

Can we stop texting when we r right next 2
each other

PRIANKA

Ok

CECILY

Bye 😂 😂

VICTORIA

Bye 🙅 🙅

Dear students:

You're holding something very special in your hands! Students come back years later and tell us they still have their seventh-grade Outdoor Education Journals!

We'll be writing in these journals for the next two weeks leading up to the trip, during the trip, and afterward, too.

Please write your name on the front cover and make sure not to lose it.

Happy writing!
Your seventh-grade English teachers

Miriam, Gabrielle

MIRIAM

Hey

So glad we r study buddies

Did u take any notes 2day

GABRIELLE

Hi!

I didn't take any today

U?

MIRIAM

No lol

GABRIELLE

Hahahahah

Soooooo

MIRIAM

Let's be good about it tomorrow k

GABRIELLE

K

MIRIAM

Who r u gonna sit with @ lunch

GABRIELLE

Prob Cece & Pri & Vic

They got really upset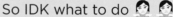

So IDK what to do

MIRIAM

Uhhhh that is hectic

I GG Mom calling me

C u tomorrow

GABRIELLE

Bye

HELP ME

VICTORIA

Guys my mom is going loony tunes again 👹👺😡😈🙅‍♀️🙇‍♀️

First she said I shouldn't go 2 outdoor ed bc it sounds dangerous 🙅‍♀️🙇‍♀️🛑⛔🚫 🚳🚵🙅‍♀️🆘

Now she thinks it'll be ok but she wants 2 request I be in a bunk w/ girls she knows bc she doesn't trust the girls in our grade 🙅‍♀️🙇‍♀️🙅‍♀️🙇‍♀️🙅‍♀️🙇‍♀️

Did u hear Sami is doing some kind of thing where she is ranking everyone based on prettiness or something 👰💃👩👩👱‍♀️ 👩👩👸

I overheard her talking about it 👧👧

Hellooooo 🔈🔉📢📣🎤🗣👂

77

VICTORIA

Where r u guys ⁉️❓⁉️

I need ur helppppppp 🆘🆘🆘🆘🆘🆘

PRIANKA

Hi sorry 😵😵😵😵

I went 2 Sage's house 2 work on poetry 📚📚

LOL we sound like dorks 🤓📖

But it was fun 😊😊😊

VICTORIA

Oh cool 👏👏

PRIANKA

So what r u going 2 do

VICTORIA

IDK 🙍🙍

She can't request bunks 😥😥😥

VICTORIA

But I really want 2 go obv

Why can't I have a normal mom 👩

PRIANKA

Are any moms normal LOL JK 😆 🤸 😆

CECILY

Hiiii sorrrryyyyy was finishing hw
📚📚📚📚

Sooooo tired 😵 😵 😫

Vic, I have an idea 💡

Why doesn't my mom talk 2 ur mom
👩👩👩

VICTORIA

Ooooh that could maybe work 🤞🤞

CECILY

They see each other @ meetings
sometimes right

VICTORIA

Yeah they do 👏 👏

GABRIELLE

Hi

Sorry

Was in the

How did u hear about the Sami thing?

VICTORIA

I overheard her in the 🚽 talking to
Hannah P

GABRIELLE

Did u tell ur mom about it

Be honest

VICTORIA

Ummmmm

Vic....

VICTORIA

I did

GABRIELLE

Y

U tell ur mom everything !!!!!!!!!!!

VICTORIA

IDK it just came out

CECILY

LOL ok 😂 😂

GABRIELLE

My mom can talk to ur mom, too, Vic

VICTORIA

K

Should I plan a moms + kids lunch or something 😳 😳 😳

PRIANKA

Ummmmmmm

CECILY

That could work 😵 😵

We find out about the play 2morrow so let me see how that goes & then get back 2 u 👩 👩 👩

Maybe we should have moms hang on their own actually

GABRIELLE

Yeah all of us bra shopping w/ moms thing was blarrrgghhh

VICTORIA

K that could work

Thx for listening 🌀 🖤 🌀 🖤

GABRIELLE

Mwah 🖤 🖤

PRIANKA

Don't stress

CECILY

4 real don't stress ☮ ☮ ☮

OMG

G   C   V   P

CECILY

Guuyyssssssssssssss 😆 😆 😆 😆 😆 😆 😆

Guesss whattttttttt 😲 😲 😲

PRIANKA

??

CECILY

I got such a fab part in the play

 What part

CECILY

The narrator 💁 💁 💁

Sharing it with Hannah F

GABRIELLE

Ohh yay 👏 👏 👏 👏

No clue what that part is or even what the play is but yay 💃 💃 💃 💃

PRIANKA

Good job, Cece 🙌 👏 👏 👏 🙌

CECILY

I am sooooooo excited 😻 😻

Cecily, Mara

C M

CECILY

I got a great part in the musical 😀

MARA

Yeah?

CECILY

Yeah the narrator

MARA

Woooooo

CECILY

So what else is up

MARA

Not much

Hiiii!!!

So excited we are co-narrators!!! Woo!

Xoxo Cecily

 I know! Same! XO Hannah

♡ xoxo

Miriam, Gabrielle

MIRIAM

Gabs

This thing with Sami 😬 😬 😬

It's kind of fun but IDK also kind of awk
😨 😱 😨 😨

GABRIELLE

What is the latest 😬 😬 😬

I am so confused 💁 💁

MIRIAM

She got this idea to rank the girls in the grade

All these categories 📓 📓

GABRIELLE

Right, yeah

MIRIAM

IDK

She's still working on it

GABRIELLE

Hmmmm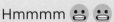

I don't know if it's mean or not

MIRIAM

IK 🙅🙅

Could go either way

GABRIELLE

In a way it's just a fun thing for her friends

But IDK

MIRIAM

U know Sami 😵 😵

GABRIELLE

Only sorta LOL 😂 😂 🤣 😂

MIRIAM

She just does what she wants

GABRIELLE

Hmmmm

What r some of the categories

MIRIAM

Can u talk after school

GABRIELLE

I have swim team practice

Even tho i am dropping out soon

But call me 2nite k

MIRIAM

K

UMMMM

VICTORIA

Guys 😬 😬 😖

I am so mad I mentioned the Sami thing 2 my mom 😒 😔 😟 😟 😤 😠 🙍‍♀️

Why am I so dumb 😟 🙁 😟

PRIANKA

What Sami thing 🙍 🙍

VICTORIA

The ranking 📓 📖

PRIANKA

I have no clue about that 🙍 🙍

It's better 2 not pay attention 2 stuff honestly 🤔 🤔

CECILY

IDK about it either really 🤔 🤔

CECILY

Just focused on the play & swim team & schoolwork 🤓 🤓

VICTORIA

Oh

GABRIELLE

IDK that much either 🤨 🤨

VICTORIA

My mom is obv speaking about it @ the 7th grade parents' meeting 😤 😒 🙄 😠 😤 😠 😤 😠 😤 😤 😠 😠 😤 😠

Why is she sooooooo embarrassing 😳 😳 😳 😳

GABRIELLE

LOL IDK 🙄 🤨 😨 😂 😂

All moms are 😇 😏 😊 🙂

Prianka, Gabrielle

PRIANKA

Gabs, we couldn't find u

Sneaking fone in bathroom 2 tell u we won't be @ lunch today

Cece & I r going w/ Vic 2 speak 2 guidance about her mom and the trip & stuff

Love u

If u get this in time meet us there

K bye

Mwah

Bye 4 real

Gabs—in case you don't see your phone, Cece & I going with Victoria to guidance to talk about her mom and the trip, etc. if you get this and want, u can meet us.
Xoxox Pri

Categories of Awesome for 7th grade girls by
Sami B. Mollinsky (this is not in a particular order)

1. Prettiness
2. Athletic ability
3. Sense of humor
4. Outgoing-ness (is that a word?)
5. Confidence
6. Sense of style
7. Most friends
8. Smarts
9. Best hair
10. Best eyes
11. Kindest
12. Best at accessorizing (this kinda goes with style)
13. Tallest
14. Friendliest with boys

What else should I add?

Vishal, Prianka

VISHAL

Yooo what is up with the girls in our grade

They r wack

PRIANKA

Huh why

VISHAL

This ranking thing Sami is doing

PRIANKA

Oh I honestly don't care

I keep tuning out when people mention it

I have a whole diff attitude this year

VISHAL

LOL ok

PRIANKA

Don't LOL me

VISHAL

Ok but what's up with the diff attitude

PRIANKA

IDK

Just kinda doing my own thing

Not getting bogged down by drama

VISHAL

Oh

R u excited for the outdoor ed trip

PRIANKA

Kinda

Not an outdoors gal tho

U

VISHAL

Kinda

PRIANKA

Ok

VISHAL

sooooooo

PRIANKA

yeahhhhhh

VISHAL

whatssssss upppppp

PRIANKA

notttttt muccccchhhhhhh

VISHAL

sorry to LOL but LOL

PRIANKA

ok gotta go 4 real now

later

Dear students:

Ready for your first journal entry?

Please answer these questions and feel free to add your own thoughts as well.

Happy writing!
Your seventh-grade English teachers

1. What are some of your initial thoughts about the trip?
2. Do you have any concerns? What are they?
3. How do you feel about leaving home?

Dear Journal,

I can't believe we have a whole book for this Outdoor Ed trip. No offense or anything. I am happy to write. But I already have a journal. It can be too much. But anyway.

So about the trip! My thoughts...um.

I am excited about it. I hope it's like Outdoor Explorers even though I know it's way more "schooly" than that. We're actually learning like science stuff.

As for my concerns...I hope the bunking is okay and I'm with at least one friend.

As for going away from home, no big deal for me. I wonder if it's a big deal for other students.

Love, Cecily

Miriam, Gabrielle

MIRIAM

So glad u sat with us @ lunch again

Where was ur crew

GABRIELLE

Same

They went 2 guidance but I didn't feel like meeting them

MIRIAM

Oh

Did you give Sami any feedback on the ranking? 🤔 🤔

GABRIELLE

No did u 😬 😬 😬

MIRIAM

No 😐 😐 😐

What can we do ????

I felt a little awk about it

She kept asking me to weigh in

MIRIAM

IDK 🤔🤔

I love her 👩‍❤️‍👩🐺

She's my bff since preschool 🐰🐰

But... 🤔🤔😬😬😬

Even tho she did add kindness 2 it ☮️✌️☮️

So maybe it's not so bad 🤔🤔

GABRIELLE

I think u have 2 say something 🤔🤔🤔

MIRIAM

IDK 😬😬😬😬😬😬

MIRIAM

I don't want to cause a rift 🫣 😶 🫣

I like my group of friends 👭👭👭

GABRIELLE

What do the Hannahs say ❓❓❓❓

MIRIAM

Nothing rlly 🤔 🤔

It's Sami's thing but she wants it to be anonymous 😶 😶

GABRIELLE

Well everyone knows it's her 🙄 🙄 😬 😬

MIRIAM

THEY DO 😲 😲❓❓😲 😲❓❓😲 😲❓❓

GABRIELLE

Yeah...

Even Victoria's mom 👱‍♀️👱‍♀️

MIRIAM

Who's Victoria ❓❓❓

GABRIELLE

She was new last year

She's nice 😬 😬

She sits @ my table @ lunch 🍽️ 🍴 🥟

MIRIAM

Oh IDK her

So what is her mom gonna do 🙄 🙄 🙄

I don't get it 🙍 🙍

GABRIELLE

IDK

She just heard about it 🙍 🙍

MIRIAM

How tho 😐 😐 😐 ❓❓

GABRIELLE

Hahaha IDK

MIRIAM

K well I gtg

Hope u sit w us @ lunch again

GABRIELLE

Xoxo 💕

Dear Journal,

Ummmmm...how am I feeling about this trip? Well, let's just hope it's better than my summer outdoor experience. I realized I'm not an outdoor gal and I'm okay with that. I have accepted who I am. I hated the hiking and I realized that I didn't need to pretend I liked it. NOT EVERYONE LIKES HIKING! It's a basic fact of life.

I'm okay with being away from home. I don't really have any concerns. I just don't want it to be torturous. A school trip is kind of exciting, though.

That's all for now.
Love, Pri

Arjun, Victoria

ARJUN

Are u really not allowed on outdoor ed

VICTORIA

No I am allowed

ARJUN

I heard your mom isn't letting u go

VICTORIA

Uggghhh how do these rumors spread

ARJUN

No idea

VICTORIA

Whatever I'm going

ARJUN

Ok

ARJUN

Are u ok

VICTORIA

Yes

Don't want to talk

Bye

From: Priscilla Melford
To: Seventh-grade Parents
Subject: Meeting

Dear parents:

As seventh-grade parent rep, I'm scheduling an additional last minute meeting for tomorrow after drop-off. Please meet in the cafeteria.

See you then,
Priscilla Melford

Sami, Gabrielle

SAMI

OMG

Ur friend Victoria is kinda crazy

GABRIELLE

????

SAMI

Her mom scheduled this whole meeting

GABRIELLE

About what

SAMI

The trip & social behavior & stuff

Did u tell her about my ranking thing

It was just for fun

108

SAMI

For my friends

GABRIELLE

I didn't tell her

She overheard u telling one of the Hannahs about it

I forgot which one

SAMI

Not sure I believe u

GABRIELLE

I promise

SAMI

Whatever

Everyone is nuts about it
😬 😬 😬 😐 😐 😐 🙄 🙄

Gonna make the trip so awk & bad
😠 😠 😠

GABRIELLE

Sami, I didn't tell anyone 😼 😼

SAMI

Fine bye

GABRIELLE

I don't understand why you don't believe me

SAMI

just seems fishy

IDK

can't explain it

GABRIELLE

how can we be real friends
if u don't believe me

SAMI

good question

● ● ●

Dear Journal,

Well, I was so excited for this trip until some recent events have me not as excited anymore. Of course there's friend drama. Will there be friend drama forever? I wonder. Probably yes. I don't want to get into it here but I'm kind of torn between two groups of friends and now there's drama between them. I'm not worried about going away from home. I loved being away this past summer. Maybe a few days deep in nature will do us some good. It's still the beginning of school and there's drama. I don't get it.

Love, Gabby

From: Yorkville Middle School Administration
To: Yorkville seventh-grade students and parents
Subject: Conduct on the trip

Dear families:

We're all looking forward to a memorable and rewarding Outdoor Education trip. We want to remind you all that social cruelty will not be tolerated. We expect the highest level of civility among all students.

Students who violate the code of conduct will be sent home immediately, and will face suspension for at least a week.

Thank you for your attention to this matter.

With best wishes,
The Yorkville Middle School Administration & Faculty

SUPER SECRET STUFFFFFFFF

SAMI

Hi guys

Super fast bc I gotta pack 4 the trip

I didn't include Gabby on this bc it's private

Should we include her friends on the rank

I think Gabs & Cecily can def make it on

Also I changed some of the categories fyi

MIRIAM

Ummmm

HANNAH P

Yeah why not

The more the better

I'll put us all on bc duh

I'm in charge LOL

I don't care who is on it tbh

I want 2 stay out of this

K whatever

sending u a pic of the list in a few

List so far

Ayelet Birnbaum – winner for prettiest & most creative

Cecily Anderson – smartest in the grade by far, no competition

Gabrielle Katz – biggest up & comer :)

Angie Kirkpatrick – friendliest, most outgoing

Sanda Yanusz – most interesting and unique

Phoebe McGellin – best fashion sense

Hannah Fletch - best voice

Eloise Modkin - prettiest name

Hannah Postel - best gymnast

Kelly O'Neal - best soccer player

Mae Revis - winner for amount of languages she knows

Becky Willard - winner for most amount of community service

Ashley Fenice - tallest

Keri Harvey - winner for most like a politician/teacher's pet (not sure if this should be on the list. thoughts?)

Note: As I went through the yearbook I realized there were lots of girls to add so I added categories but the winner of the whole thing will be someone that gets points in every category

Also: People should not find this mean. If we made a LOSER LIST that would be mean... LOL. I wouldn't do that.

I don't think. :)

PS Not everyone can be on it, it's not how it works, I get being inclusive but whatevs. This isn't that kind of thing.

PPS: For example obvs Miriam is one of my BFFs but she's all around amazing and doesn't fit into a category. Not everyone does. Just how it is.

Cecily, Prianka, Victoria, Gabrielle

CECILY

I can't believe they're letting us use on the bus

PRIANKA

Prob bc they want it to be quiet LOL

GABRIELLE

True

VICTORIA

My mom is texting me every 20 min to check in 🐺🐺😒😑

GABRIELLE

OMG, Vic

How do u deal with this ❓❓❓❓

VICTORIA

IDK 😳😒🙄🤔😂

She is just wacky pants

CECILY

Sorry, Vic 😐😐😐

Hopefully she will chill 🙍‍♀️🙍‍♀️

VICTORIA

Hopefully Sami doesn't dye my hair in my sleep or something 😳😳🙄🙄🤔😆

117

GABRIELLE

LOL no

PRIANKA

She's kinda psycho, Gabs 🤔 🤔 🤔

GABRIELLE

She's not that bad 4 real 😼

Her list is all nice stuff, nothing mean ☮ ☮

U guys just want to hate on it 😕 😕 😕 😕

CECILY

IDK about that 😬 😬 😬 😐 😐 😐

GABRIELLE

Ok guys 👧 👧

Can we not do this 🙏 🙏 🙏

CECILY

Fine

PRIANKA

Cece, what's up w/ u & Mara 🤔 🤔 🤔

PRIANKA

U barely talk

CECILY

We talk

IDK

We're busy w/ diff stuff

VICTORIA

Do u think the teachers listened 2 my mom
& we will all be in a bunk together

CECILY

No I don't 😐 😐

Didn't they already say no 🙄 🙄 ??

VICTORIA

Kinda 🤦

GABRIELLE

It is supposed to be random assignments

For bonding or whatever

Hmph

Don't worry, Vic 🙇🙇

It'll be good 👍👍👏🙌

Do u guys feel like you are on a repeat of your summer trip? 😂😂

I feel like it'll be diff

More educational 🤓🤓

Same

K going 2 work on memorizing my lines 🤓

Going 2 nap 😴😴😴

& I'll stare out the window 🚌🚌🚎🚋
& pray it's not like our summer trip
😒😒😅😅

I'll just sit here fretting LOL 😕😳😐🙍😦

121

Dear students,

Please make sure you follow all the instructions in this letter.

Go outside on the porch. Take a deep breath. Hold it.
Exhale. Smell the beautiful fresh air. Take notice of
all the nature around you. We are here to unwind, to
bond as a community, to appreciate our world and our
environment, and to take stock of our patterns and
behaviors. We are here to grow, to truly become the
people we want to be, to start the new school year on
the right foot.

Go back inside. Introduce yourself to your fellow
bunkmates if you do not know them. Say hello to your
high school chaperones. They were once seventh graders
on this trip. They have much wisdom to share.

Unpack. Make your bed. Get settled.

Please meet in the main building, down the hill at five.

We'll be waiting for you.

Yours truly,
The seventh-grade faculty

WAHHHHHHH

VICTORIA

Guysssssss I'm not with anyone I know

We have to give phones to the hs chaperone in 1 min

I am so sad

I want 2 go homeeeeeeee

Gabs—soooooooo happy we're in the same bunk. This is a sign from the universe that we are meant to be BFF. Xoxo Miriam

I am happy, too. Sami was crying, though! Did you see? Because she's not in a bunk w/ u or the Hannahs or Eloise?

Yeah. I think so. I didn't get to talk to her yet.

Is this starting soon? Why is our bunk the first one in this building and why are we not allowed to talk?

Ha! No idea.

Dear students,

Now that we've had our first activity,
we'd like you to write about it. Please
describe the trust fall and how you felt.
If you finish early, please describe your
view from the porch. What do you see?
What do you hear? What do you smell?
Use all your senses.

HAPPY WRITING!

Dear Journal,

That trust fall was insane!!!! I had to hold Anthony Mawslin. I have never even talked to him before and there I was holding his back. It was crazy. At least we didn't drop him. But seriously I was doing most of the work. Kevin Teak was helping, too, but not that much. Everyone else was all squeamish and weird, like they had one finger on Anthony and weren't really holding him. I honestly feel kind of empowered now, and definitely closer to Anthony. I guess it wasn't possible to get farther from him. We never talked before!

Love, Prianka

Dear Journal,

Okay. Wow. I was the one being held up in the trust fall exercise and it was one of the scariest things of my whole entire life. The teachers picked the person in the group to fall and Ms. Noemp picked me. I was kind of flattered at first but then freaked out. How was I really going to trust my group? I didn't know anyone in it! Well, that's not true. Brian Goldfarb and I were in a playgroup together as babies but that doesn't really count. So anyway, I climbed up the ladder, and when I looked down I saw everyone standing there, arms outstretched and sort of interlinked like some kind of human quilt. The ropes instructor guy told me to turn around, so I did, and then I hesitated a minute and then I fell back and they caught me! There I was—totally held up by my peers! It was kind of an amazing experience. I guess we really do hold each other up. Sounds cheesy but true. I'm hungry now.

Love, Cecily

Dear Gabby,

I know we're supposed to be writing in our journals now and I technically am writing in my journal but I'm writing a note to you instead. I am really upset about what happened. I feel like I was punished and separated from all my friends on this trip because of your friend Victoria and her mom. Honestly, I wasn't going to rank everyone in the grade—we have a huge grade of over 200 people, I don't even know everyone! Also, it wasn't for everyone to see. Don't you get how this was blown totally out of proportion? It's crazy. And you and Cecily are on it! It's a huge compliment. I really like you guys. Well I like you. I don't know Cecily that well but I know she is super smart.

Anyway, I think you need to go explain to the teachers with me since you're friends with

Victoria. And you need to tell them that this was not what they thought. I don't deserve to be punished. I'm all alone on this trip now. And my parents are mad at me.

I want you to be friends with us but I'm not sure you can stay friends with us because I don't know about your loyalty. Are you a real, true friend to stand up for me? I know we just became friends recently but I thought you were a real friend and that's why I shared the ranking with you.

Please write back and let me know. I think we should go talk to the teachers after dinner tonight. I hope you're going to say yes, otherwise I don't know what we can do.

Love, Sami

Dear Journal,

How do I get into these messes? The trust fall was actually really cool but I was too stressed to even enjoy it because of all the other drama. I'll quickly summarize: Anya Riak was the one falling and she was super nervous. She stood up there for like ten minutes before even leaning back. And we just stood there ready to catch her. Maybe she had to know that we were really there for her. I'm not sure. It was a cool experience. I'm glad I wasn't the one who had to fall. I'm also glad Victoria was in my group because she was so upset about everything and at least we had a few minutes to talk face-to-face. Ugh. Anyway, I need to close my eyes and take deep breaths now.

Love, Gabs

Dear Cece,

Do you know that you're on the ranking? I am, too. This is a big compliment. I'm not supposed to say anything but you're on it for being the smartest in the grade by far. Obviously I agree. But come on, why is this rank thing so crazy? Can we discuss it? Don't hate.

Love, Gabs

Date: _____

Table: _____

Names of students at your table: _____
_____
_____

Amount of food waste: _____
_____
_____

Reflections: _____
_____
_____
_____

G-Meet me by the bathroom in 5 minutes. -S

Guys, I'm writing this on the back
of a napkin in the third stall in the
bathroom. I think I need to leave early.
Everyone is being so mean to me because
they're saying I blabbed to my mom and
got Sami in trouble. I hate my bunk
and my table and I miss you guys and
I want to go home. If I disappear, you'll
know why. Love, VM

Dear Journal,

I hate this trip. I hate the kids in my grade. I hate my mom for making such a big deal out of everything all the time. I hate everything. What would my life be like if I had a different mom? Imagine who I could be and what I could accomplish. Why are some people born with terrible moms and some with great ones? I don't get it. Is there a reason for these things?

Love, Victoria Melford, the miserable

Gabs, I don't want to put any of this in writing. It is getting out of hand. I can discuss with you later. Love, Cece

Please write your reflections about the
incident on this sheet of paper.
We will discuss it when you're finished.

I believe I was caught in the middle of
something that wasn't my fault. I'm sorry
it caused pain and disrupted the 7th
grade trip. That was never my intention.
I didn't expect my mom to tell people
about Sami's list. —Victoria

Please write your reflections about the
incident on this sheet of paper.
We will discuss it when you're finished.

My list was a private thing among my friends
and wasn't meant to hurt anyone's feelings. It
was just a funny activity. I am sorry I disrupted
the trip and got mad at Victoria. I didn't mean
to be rude. I think we should be allowed to do
our own private stuff without a million parents
and kids getting involved. -Sami

Dear Miriam,

I can't believe you are totally taking Sami's side here. I know we just became friends but I was excited about getting to know you better and your friends, too. I enjoyed sitting at your table. I don't understand why you are blaming me for this whole thing with Sami's ranking and the Victoria drama. Honestly I thought you had more of an independent mind and didn't need to follow everything Sami does.

Love, Gabby

Gabby and friends:
Stop talking to us. You're annoying. You're ruining this trip. I'm taking Gabby and Cecily off the ranking now. You had good qualities but you're making everyone miserable. Please just stop before we get in more trouble.
Sami

Well, this trip has become a nightmare. Everything went crazy with Sami and Victoria and Gabby and now those girls hate us, not that we were that close anyway. But whatever. I guess Gabby wanted to be friends with them. TBH, I think she still does. Who knows. Ever since our summer trip Gabby is bored with our group of friends but she won't admit it. I am ready to go home and move on from this nightmare. Love, Cecily

Dear Journal,

I am patting myself on the back because I did not get involved in the drama on this trip. I hung out with Sage (PBFF—poetry best friend forever) and Vishal a little bit and that was it. I refuse to be dragged into the Sami drama. No thank you. The trip was great.

Love, Pri

Victoria—you okay? —Arjun

No, not okay. Hate everything. Bye.

Birds seen on this trip:

Laughing gull

Red-tailed hawk

House sparrow

Herring gull

Eastern bluebird

Leaves seen so far:
Ginkgo
Beech
Sugar maple
Elm

Tree observations:
Green
Fluffy
Looming
Protective
Surrounding
Covering
Shading

WAHHHH

CECILY

Soooooo tired from the trip & we have a swim meet today 💤 💤 💤 😵‍💫 😵‍💫 😵‍💫

GABRIELLE

IK may bail

VICTORIA

Pls don't bail 😠 😕 🧕 🙁

Need 2 talk 2 u guys 🗣 🗣 🗣

Sami still harassing me 🙁 😩 🙁 😩

PRIANKA

Oyyy 🙀 😾 😾

Sage taught me that expression

Her gma speaks yiddish to her ✡️ ✡️ 🕎 〰️

PRIANKA

So cool right 😎 👍

GABRIELLE

CECILY

I gtg guys 👍 👋 💁

Cu later @ swim or school 👋 👋

Don't worry, Vic—we r here 4 u

GABRIELLE

Yes 👍 👍 👍

VICTORIA

K

Pls protect me 🙌 🙏 🙇

143

UMMMMMM???

GABRIELLE

Ok I know no side chats but

What is up w/ Vic

She's going nuts again

CECILY

IDK Sami is really mean

GABRIELLE

Honestly she's not that bad

That whole rank thing was just something
for her little group

It all went

Can't we take a step back here & look clearly

I mean Cece u were on it, too

Didn't that make u even a little happy

CECILY

Ummmmm not really

I don't need Sami's approval of me

It's kind of sad that u need it, Gabs

PRIANKA

Staying out of drama

Sorry

Bye

Prianka has left the chat

OMG & Pri, too 😴😴😴

She acts like she's better than us bc she's all into poetry

CECILY

Stop, Gabs 🛑🛑

Ur the one who needs to take a step back and understand what's going on 😕😒🤨

GABRIELLE

Ugh now ur turning against me, too 🤨😒😠😒

Grrrrr 🙅🙍🙍

Bye 🖐🖐

CECILY

Love you! 💘💞💗🤍

Dear Ms. Brickfeld:

I'm leaving you this note in your box because I couldn't find you in the guidance office. I'd like to set up a meeting with you to discuss some personal matters.

Thank you,

Gabrielle Katz

Leaving notes in all of your lockers so you don't wonder where I am. Meeting Ms. Brickfeld @ lunch.

Xox Gabs

Cecily—please help me. Meet me in the first-floor bathroom as soon as you can. Sami keeps glaring at me. I think she's spreading all kinds of rumors. Please help. —VM

From: Yorkville Middle School Administration
To: Yorkville seventh-grade students and parents
Subject: Troubling behavior

Dear families:

It's come to my attention that there was some troubling behavior on the seventh-grade trip. It appears that it's still going on at school. I'd like to schedule a last-minute meeting for tomorrow at 7 p.m. to go over our code of conduct and school policies. Threatening and cruel behavior will not be tolerated.

With best wishes,
Edward Carransey

You must be the change you want to see in the world.
—Gandhi

From: Evelyn Brickfeld
To: Gabrielle Katz
Subject: Our meeting

Dear Gabby,

I hope you feel a little better after our meeting today. Feel free to come back anytime. Please keep me updated on the situation.

Ms. Brickfeld

Laughter is the brush that sweeps away the cobwebs of your heart. —Mort Walker

Dear Gabs,

So glad you came to find me in the 3rd-floor bathroom. Thanks for going to Ms. Brickfeld to talk to her, too. I think the more people I have on my side, the better. It's obvious that Victoria and her mom are crazy. Sit with us from now on. You'll be way happier. I need to show you the updated list. And honestly, I feel like the swim team will just take away from hangout time. Who wants to swim in the winter anyway?

Xoxoxoxoxo Sami

From: Diana Katz
To: Elizabeth Anderson, Manjula Basak
Subject: Our girls

Ladies,

Hi! How's everything? Sorry I have been so woefully out of touch. The beginning of the year always makes me crazy. Seems like our girls are a little nutty, too. What have you been hearing? I'm worried Gabs is getting mixed up with the wrong group of kids. Can we have coffee?

Love you,
D

Sami,
Cool. I don't know where I'm sitting for
lunch but glad the air is clear between us.
Love, Gabs

Just sit with us. Why are you being so
weird? :)

Ha! Ok. Gotta stop passing notes.
This sub keeps looking at me.

Subs are lame. But ok. Bye.

FRIENDS

V G C P

VICTORIA

Guys so glad we r all here

Let's text instead of talk since all these girls around us could listen

GABRIELLE

Well they could read over our shoulders, too, LOL

CECILY

Gabs!

GABRIELLE

What? Just saying

PRIANKA

Whatever

Anyway here 4 u, Vic

PRIANKA

What's up

VICTORIA

Sending u a pic of this note I found in my locker

Do u recognize handwriting

CAN U PLEASE STOP BEING SO ANNOYING? NONE OF THIS IS A BIG DEAL. YOU'RE MAKING THIS HARDER ON YOURSELF. OK? EVERYONE IS GOING TO HATE YOU SOON. JUST STOP.

PRIANKA

No idea

I think this whole thing just needs to blow over

PRIANKA

I don't even think Sami is doing the ranking anymore

Btw, Cece, why did Mara drop out of swim team

CECILY

IDK

I think she's doing some weekly community service thing

PRIANKA

Oh

VICTORIA

Anyway back to my drama 😬 😬 😬

GABRIELLE

I agree w/ Pri ☮ ☮

Just ignore & it will pass

Rip up the note & move on

VICTORIA

But why is this even happening again

It's like the thing @ Vishal's party last year
w/ the mystery texter 😵 😵

PRIANKA

No this is just dumb drama 🙄 🙄 🙄

CECILY

Pri is right 💔 💔

We gotta listen to Michelle Obama

VICTORIA

???

CECILY

When they go low we go high

VICTORIA

Oh right 🐱 😀

VICTORIA

But still

Feels stressful

CECILY

IK

GABRIELLE

K guys

Time 2 🛏️ 🛏️

VICTORIA

👧 👧

Gabrielle, Sami

GABRIELLE

Why did u leave Victoria that note

SAMI

What note

GABRIELLE

In her locker

SAMI

IDK what u mean

GABRIELLE

Ok

I know u left Victoria that note

Cecily, Gabrielle

CECILY

OMG, Gabs 😬 😬 😼 😼

Sorry picked up ur phone by mistake

U left it on the bleachers

I saw text from Sami 🙄 🙄

She left Vic that note 📝 📝 📝

& u knew it was her ? ? ? ? ?

GABRIELLE

Omg 😬 😬 😬

Why r u reading my phone

CECILY

I picked it up by mistake 🙄 🙄 🙄

CECILY

Why don't you lock your screen

GABRIELLE

UGH IDK 😬 😬 😬

U DIDN'T HAVE TO READ IT

This is OOC 😱 😮 😵 🤫 🙅

From: Gabrielle Katz
To: Cecily Anderson, Prianka Basak, Victoria Melford
Subject: Us

Dear Cecily, Prianka, and Victoria,

I don't even know how to write this. I told Coach Wembly that I'm dropping out of the swim team.

I just need a break from our little group. We've been BFF since before we were even born (except for Victoria) and I think I just need some space. I still love you guys but it feels like I want to do different stuff from you all. I just want to branch out a little bit. I felt really good about myself when I made so many new friends over the summer camping and I feel good about making new friends at school, too. I think it's okay to have more than one group, especially since we have been BFF for literally forever. I hope you'll understand.

Love, Gabs

WIGO???

V P C

VICTORIA

Um

Is it time for another intervention

PRIANKA

LOL no

Just let it be

No friend drama

How many times have I told u guys this

VICTORIA

Ok but it's awk & sad

163

PRIANKA

Did u ever hear the thing that goes if u love someone set them free?

It's kinda like that

CECILY

Too busy 2 deal

Need 2 practice play lines

VICTORIA

K

Friendships by Prianka Basak

Things are shifting
But I feel calm
Friendships are changing
But I accept it
People try and make drama
But I stay away
The only thing I can control
Is myself
I stand by that
I am loyal to my principles
Strong
Fierce
Independent
Confident
No time
for
anything
less

From: Sami Mollinsky
To: Miriam Seelbaum, Hannah Postel, Hannah Fletch, Gabrielle Katz, Eloise Modkin
Subject: WOOO

So excited you're all sleeping over Friday. Gabby's first sleepover with us! Woo! We'll continue secret project that will not be named. Bring snacks and your comfiest pj's. Hugs! Sami

From: Elizabeth Anderson
To: Diana Katz, Manjula Basak
Subject: RE: Our girls

Hi, ladies,

So glad we got to meet for coffee. I love our plan for the weekend after Thanksgiving. Hopefully we'll have some snow. Let's keep it a surprise for the girls. We'll keep them close whether they like it or not. :) Question is: What should we do about Victoria? Are we being too exclusive?

Love, Elizabeth

JOSEPH AND THE AMAZING TECHNICOLOR DREAMCOAT

REHEARSAL SCHEDULE

Monday: 3:30–4:30
Tuesday: 3:30–5:30
Wednesday: 3:30–4:30
Thursday: 3:30–6:00
Friday: work on lines @ home

Go go go Joseph!
Ms. Golota & the theater department staff

Dear Journal,

Technically I'm supposed to be writing a rough draft in here on my reflections of the school trip but I can't focus on it. The only thing that is on my mind is what's happening with my friends. I guess that ties into the trip, though. I just feel like I'm being pulled in two different directions. I want to be friends with Sami, Miriam, Eloise, and the Hannahs but I also love my cozy, comfy little group where they get me and they know me. I want to branch out so badly but I also don't. It doesn't seem possible to be in two different groups especially when Sami is the leader of one. Who knew she had so much power? She definitely didn't last year. I don't even know where this has come from. This feels terrible and stressful and I know I hurt my friends' feelings. Also I was excited about the swim team so I don't even know why I dropped out. I just feel like I want to do different stuff but I don't even know what I want to do. I feel like Sami is definitely pushing me into stuff but I still want to be friends with Miriam and the Hannahs and their group. I wonder if that makes me the worst person ever.

Love, Gabby

- -

From: Sally B. Wembly
To: Yorkville Swim Team
Subject: Our commitment

Dear swimmers:

I know the season can be long and YOU'RE ALL DOING SO GREAT! I am so grateful for your dedication to our team.

Unfortunately, a few of our swimmers have dropped off the swim team. I encourage you to stay committed.

Here's your Sally B. Wembly approved inspirational quote: "I wouldn't say anything is impossible. I think that everything is possible as long as you put your mind to it and put the work and time into it." —Michael Phelps

PS I was reminded that I never responded to the answers about my middle name...no one guessed it...it's BEATRICE!!! :)

Go Yorkville!
Coach Sally B. Wembly

FEEELINGSSSSSS

VICTORIA

I'm not counting this as a side chat since Gabs has basically decided to leave the group 😭 😭 🐺

Obv I'm super hurt by this

CECILY

I know

We r, too 😩 😩 🐱

We've been friends since before we were even born

PRIANKA

Yes

CECILY

That's all u have to say, Pri

😬 😬 😬 🙄 🙄 😾 😾

PRIANKA

Told u ☮️ ☮️

Not getting involved

⛔ ⛔ ⛔ ⛔ ⛔ ⛔ ⛔

CECILY

But this is Gabs 😬 😬 😬

CECILY

Our bff

PRIANKA

IK

She'll come around

CECILY

U r being so weird, Pri

PRIANKA

Sorry

I gtg

Prianka has left the chat

VICTORIA

What is up w/ her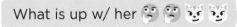

CECILY

No clue

Everyone is wacky pants

4 real

CECILY

I gtg study play lines & do hw

VICTORIA

Don't goooo

CECILY

I'm sorry, Vic

Pls don't stress

It'll all work out

Mwah

VICTORIA

Mwah

From: Jane Marburn
To: Diana Katz
Subject: Gabby's behavior

Dear Ms. Katz:

I'm writing because Gabby has been exhibiting some unusual behavior lately. She's chatting incessantly during class and does not seem to pay attention to warnings and discipline. She received a check minus today for poor behavior and eye rolling. This seems very unlike her, and it's troubling. I wanted to touch base and see if anything is going on at home. Please feel free to email back or call the main office.

Thank you,
Ms. Marburn
English teacher

Imagination is more important than knowledge.
—Albert Einstein

Gabrielle, Mom

MOM

Gabs, please come down and talk to me

GABRIELLE

Busy

MOM

This isn't a choice

Come down now

GABRIELLE

I'm doing hw 📚📖📚📖

MOM

Immediately or I take your phone away for a week

GABRIELLE

Coming

UGGGGHHHHHH

GABRIELLE

Guys I got in trouble for poor behavior in Ms. Marburn's class

SAMI

Don't worry she's a witch

GABRIELLE

My mom is so mad

MIRIAM

Oh sorry, Gabs

GABRIELLE

I'm not allowed to go out w u guys 4 Halloween

ELOISE

BLARGHHHHHHHHH

HANNAH P

Yeah that stinks

HANNAH F

I get in trouble every day tho

I'm over it

GABRIELLE

Yeah but my mom isn't over it

SAMI

So annoying

This school is too strict

At my cousin's school they call teachers by first names and it's super chill

ELOISE

Jellllyyyyyyyyyyy

GABRIELLE

That sounds cool

SAMI

Don't show anyone those lists btw

SAMI

Looking @ u, Gabs 👀 👀 👀

GABRIELLE

I won't

Promise 🙏 ✌️

SAMI

Looks like Ayelet Birnbaum is our winner of our girl ranking system 💯 🏆

Let's be friends with her 👰👰 👰👰

MIRIAM

This is awk now, Sam 🤨 🤨 😼 😼

SAMI

No it's not 🙄 🙄 🙄

I mean we could've made ourselves the winners 🙄 🙄 🏆

But we didn't

SAMI

& I never made the Loser List LOL

Maybe next time LOL 😛🤣😛🤣😝🤣

HANNAH F

Honestly this is getting too weird 😲😲

HANNAH P

Yeah ur taking it way too seriously
🙄🙄🙄

ELOISE

I am so confused by this TBH 🤷‍♀️🤷‍♀️🤷‍♀️🤷‍♀️

SAMI

Whatever guys 🙄🙄🙄

It's just a fun thing 😝😛😝

Ugh 😬😬

GABRIELLE

I gtg 🙌🙌🙌

GABRIELLE

Mom is limiting phone time

MIRIAM

Bye, Gabs

From: Elizabeth Anderson
To: Diana Katz, Manjula Basak
Subject: Our trip

Hi, ladies:

Okay, we're all booked! Weekend after Thanksgiving! We'll plan to leave Friday morning no later than ten so we can get to Millcreek Mountain House for lunch. Then the girls will go to the "teen camp" they have, free of charge! The three of us will get massages. We can do snowshoeing—pray for snow! There's tons to do. Check the website. Really looking forward to this.

I think it's for the best that Priscilla has her sister in town. I love Victoria but I'm not totally sure Priscilla loves us. :) Oh well. I'm glad we included them. When should we tell the girls?

Love, Elizabeth

Gabs, I miss you. I see you in the hallway with Sami and them and at lunch and I have to be honest, it kind of breaks my heart. What can we do? Love, Cecily

Cecily, it's nothing you did. I just felt the need to branch out. I felt stuck with you guys and you never wanted me to rotate tables. I wanted that feeling I had on the camping trip of being friends with a lot of people. I don't want to feel trapped with just a few. I think I am getting more social as I get older and I like that. I feel like I am more outgoing all of a sudden and less nervous. I still love you, duh. We have different interests now. We are growing up and we are different than we used to be. I just need some space. I want to have other friends. It's just like you doing the play and how Pri is all into poetry with Sage now. This is my way to meet new people. Love, Gabs

Yeah, but you're not even friends with us. You just ignore us. We can have different groups of friends. You're right, I really like the cast of Joseph. That doesn't mean I don't talk to Pri and Vic. This is so silly. Why did you need to distance yourself from us entirely? We're all really hurt, especially Victoria.

You don't get it. You guys never let anyone branch out. So I had to totally distance otherwise I would have been stuck. I'm sorry but it's true. You guys are only into our little group.

That is not true and now you're doing the same thing. You left the swim team. Think about it. I was able to be friends with you guys and Mara, too. Take a look at yourself. I can't believe we're going to go trick-or-treating without you. :(

I don't want to go trick-or-treating anyway. I wanted to go to the party in Sami's neighborhood. Anyway, I'm sorry about all of this but I need to expand my horizons.

From: Edward Carransey
To: Eric Mollinsky, Anne Mollinsky, Andrew Seelbaum, Janet Seelbaum, Evelyn Postel, Marc Postel, George Fletch, Nina Fletch, Diana Katz, Douglas Katz, Ines Modkin, and Pierre Modkin
Subject: Meeting

Dear Parents:

Some very disturbing behavior has come to our attention. Please meet in my office at 9 a.m. tomorrow with your children.

Mr. Carransey

You must be the change you want to see in the world.
—Gandhi

OMG

SAMI

U guys 😟 😔 😑 🙄 😫 😫

Someone let that sheet get out
😫 😫 😫 😫 😫 😫

And someone found it 😟 😟

And brought it to Mr. C 😦 😮 😦 😮

Who was it ????

Tell me now 😠 😠 😠

HANNAH P

Not me

HANNAH F

Me neither

ELOISE

Same

MIRIAM

I never even had the sheet 📃📃📃📃

GABRIELLE

Same

U said u were keeping the only copy

SAMI

I sent u guys the pic

Anyone could've emailed it 2 someone

& printed it out

MIRIAM

We didn't 🚫🚫

SAMI

U r all lying 💁💁💁

Now we have to go to a meeting with Mr. C
& our parents 😡😡😡

MIRIAM

I know 😬😬

MIRIAM

So upset 😭😭😭😿😿

GABRIELLE

Me too 😿😿😿😿😿😿

SAMI

Whatever we'll just deny it
🙍🙍🙍😆😛😜😬

HANNAH P

IDK about that 🤔🤔

HANNAH F

Yeah let's just be honest ☮️☮️✌️

& move on 🛑🛑

SAMI

Guys this is serious 😨😱😨😱

ELOISE

Wahhhhhh 😨😨😨

MIRIAM

We know 😩😩😩😿😿

From: Diana Katz
To: Elizabeth Anderson, Manjula Basak
Subject: Gabby

Ladies,

Gabby has gotten in serious trouble at school. Somehow she found herself mixed up with this Girl Rank thing. Do you know about it? I'm so disappointed in her. I've banned her from Halloween and now I may need to cancel this trip. Not sure she deserves a luxurious weekend away. I'll keep you updated.

X Diana

Arjun, Victoria

ARJUN

Where have u been

Ur so quiet

VICTORIA

I'm here

Just trying to stay out of drama

ARJUN

Um

Do I cause drama

VICTORIA

Not really no LOL

Just trying to lie low

ARJUN

Ur funny

ARJUN

Ok

What r u doing 4 Halloween

VICTORIA

Trick or treating w/ my friends

U?

ARJUN

Same

Prianka Basak
Poetry Elective

Sometimes I wake up
In the middle of the night
And I can't get back
To

Sleep
It's as if a little
Animal
Is running away with my sleep
Snatching it
Like a scarf
And then I'm wide-eyed
Awake
Staring at the ceiling
I wish
That little animal
Would return
With
My
Sleep

Sage, Prianka

S   P

SAGE

Hey 😀 😀 😀

U wanna go 2 the movies Saturday

PRIANKA

Let me double-check my schedule

LOL JK

I'm free 😀 😀 😀

Sure

SAGE

 ✓

PRIANKA

What are u doing for Halloween

SAGE

Soooo not a Halloween girl

U

PRIANKA

I always do trick or treating in my hood w/ my friends 🏃🏃 🏃🏃 🏃🏃

If u change ur mind u can come

SAGE

Haha k 😂 😂

From: Edward Carransey
To: Eric Mollinsky, Anne Mollinsky, Andrew Seelbaum, Janet Seelbaum, Evelyn Postel, Marc Postel, George Fletch, Nina Fletch, Diana Katz, Douglas Katz, Ines Modkin, and Pierre Modkin
Subject: Follow-up

Dear all,

Following up on today's meeting.

1. Students will have a two-day at-home suspension for social cruelty.
2. Students will write an apology letter to the grade that will be read aloud in each homeroom.
3. Students will choose one of the school's ongoing community service projects and devote twenty after-school hours to it.
4. Students have lost computer privileges for the remainder of the trimester.
5. It has been advised that students lose phone privileges at home for at least a week as well. That is up to the families.

Please let me know if you have any questions. We are committed to ensuring that Yorkville Middle School is a kind, welcoming place, and we have a zero-tolerance policy for social cruelty.

With best wishes,
Mr. Carransey

You must be the change you want to see in the world.
—Gandhi

Miriam, Gabrielle

MIRIAM

R u there

GABRIELLE

Yeah but losing tonight

My mom said to say goodbye to it 4 a while

MIRIAM

Same

Can I ask u something

GABRIELLE

Sure

MIRIAM

Can I sit w u & ur friends now

My mom wants me 2 stay away from Sami 4 a while

GABRIELLE

Really?

Wow

MIRIAM

Yeah

She thinks we need space

I kinda agree

Sami was also going to make a loser list

Just fyi

GABRIELLE

Wow   🤨

Sure u can sit w us 💺💺💺

If they even still like me 😨

MIRIAM

Obv when we r back from suspension

MIRIAM

Right ughhh

GABRIELLE

K gotta hand over

MIRIAM

K bye

Dear Mom,

I know you said to write you a letter describing what happened so you could understand it better but the thing is, I don't even know how to explain it. It was just like this thing that happened kind of out of nowhere. Victoria's mom found out about the ranking thing because Victoria overheard Sami and then Victoria's mom told people. But then Sami didn't stop. In her mind it wasn't even that bad. And sometimes when I think about it I wonder if it is that bad. It wasn't supposed to be public. I mean, it's not the nicest thing but is it the worst thing? I don't know. Anyway, I'm sorry it got so out of hand. I am going to go back to sitting with my old friends. I think it's better that way. You also asked me what I can do going forward and it sounds cheesy, but I'm going to focus on kindness. I'm sorry I disappointed you.

Love, Gabby

Guys, I am in so much trouble. Suspended for two days, phone confiscated, who knows when I'll be able to go out. I'm surprised I was even allowed to walk this around the corner to Cece's mailbox. Ugh. I am miserable. I knew Sami was bad news but this has gotten crazy.

Sorry, Gabs. We love you even though you abandoned us. The thing is, will Sami and them hold on to their popularity status? No clue. Btw the play is less than two months away! Will you please come see me and sit in the front row and clap? :)

Not to pat myself on the back too much but I told you to stay out of the drama. For the future, always listen to Prianka Basak the Extraordinary. Xoxo

I can't even discuss this since I think it's mostly my fault for blabbing to my mom. I just want it to be over.

From: Gabrielle Katz
To: Edward Carransey
Subject: Idea

Dear Mr. Carransey:

I've done a great deal of thinking over my two-day suspension. I have an idea of something I can do to help improve the school. It's called a Kindness Rock Garden. Have you seen these before? I didn't make it up but I think it would be awesome. We could set it up under the trees in the courtyard. All we need is some smooth rocks and colorful permanent markers. I am happy to discuss this with you in person.

Thank you for your consideration,
Gabby Katz

You're never fully dressed without a smile. —Annie

Dear Gabs,

Good luck on your first day back. I know it's been tough. I'm proud of you for staying true to yourself. Never forget how much I love you.

Mom

Putting notes in all your lockers. Can Miriam sit with us @ lunch today? Will you be my friends again? Pretty please.

I guess so. LOL. Sure. Again, no drama for me.

Sure. Welcome back.

Does she even want to sit with me? Doubt it.

Yes, Vic. She's not like Sami.

I thought you didn't think Sami was so bad?

I don't know. But Miriam is nice for real. I promise.

Okay. Fine.

Gabrielle, Miriam

So glad u sat w/ us today

MIRIAM

Me 2

Ur friends r nice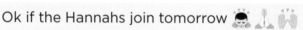

Ok if the Hannahs join tomorrow

GABRIELLE

Sure

Can we all fit

MIRIAM

We can squeeze

GABRIELLE

K

GABRIELLE

How is Sami doing

MIRIAM

Her mom is worried about her

She was suspended from school

Not everyone knows that

GABRIELLE

Yeah I didn't know

I still feel like she didn't mean it to be as big a deal as it became but it def wasn't right

MIRIAM

No not at all

She takes things too far sometimes

GABRIELLE

Yeah

GABRIELLE

& I started to see her true colors

Like she is deep down kind of a mean person

I'm sorry to say that but do u KWIM

MIRIAM

IKWYM 🫣🫣

GABRIELLE

I'm glad u get it ☮️☮️☮️☮️

MIRIAM

& I'm glad this whole thing is behind us

& that we're friends

GABRIELLE

TBH I feel the SAME 🤍🤍🤍🤍

Going to meet with Mr. C during lunch to discuss my idea. Be nice to Miriam & the Hannahs. xoxo G

What is your idea? Out of loop again. —Pri

IDK either!

Same! Fill us in after, Gabs.

Mama Basak, Mama Anderson, Mamacita, Gabrielle, Prianka, Cecily

MAMA BASAK

Hi girls & moms

MAMA ANDERSON

Hi

MAMACITA

Hiiiiiiii

GABRIELLE

WIGO

PRIANKA

IDK

CECILY

Ummmm

MAMA ANDERSON

We wanted 2 surprise you girls

MAMA BASAK

We r going on a trip after Thanksgiving

MAMACITA

To Millcreek Mountain House

Google it

MAMA ANDERSON

Teen camp and...

MAMA BASAK

Hiking, spa, s'mores, tea, snowshoeing, ice skating

Will be a blast

GABRIELLE

Is this 4 real

MAMA ANDERSON

Yes!

CECILY

I am soooooo confused

PRIANKA

TBH SAMEEEEEEEEEE

MAMA ANDERSON

LOL

Calm down

MAMACITA

Just be ready @ 10 am Friday morning
after Thanksgiving

GABRIELLE

Ok

PRIANKA

CECILY

MAMA ANDERSON

Anyone want 2 say thank u

Ha sorry

Thank u

PRIANKA

Thankkkkk uuuuuuuu

CECILY

Thank u

Very excited

MAMACITA

& fyi we invited Victoria & Priscilla

But they have family in town

CECILY

Ok 👍

UMMM

CECILY

Srsly WIGO 🙍🙍 ❓❓❓

CECILY

My mom never did this with Ingrid & friends

GABRIELLE

But she isn't bff with their moms like w/ our moms 🙍🙍🙍🙍🙍

CECILY

That's true

PRIANKA

Still tho WIGO ❓❓❓

GABRIELLE

IDK no idea

CECILY

Whatevs it sounds super fun

PRIANKA

Totes 🐤🐤🐤

Just googled

Really pumped about the tea &
🍪🍪🍪🍪 @ 4 pm every day

GABRIELLE

OMG whoa 😨😮😨😨

Me 2 👣👣👣👣 🐤🐤

CECILY

Guyssssssss this is gonna be soooooo fun
🎉🎐🎉🎈🎆🎇

Do we have our own room 🤔🤔

GABRIELLE

IDK 💁💁

PRIANKA

Let's ask the mothers

& report back on our findings

GABRIELLE

Let's not write about this in shared notebook 📖 📓 📕 📓

Even tho Vic was invited don't want her 2 feel bad ☮️ ☮️

PRIANKA

True ✅

Good point ✅

CECILY

Love u guys 🤍 🤍 🤍 🤍

Sooooo excited 🎉 🎉 🎉 🎉 🎉 🎉

WANT TO HELP SPREAD KINDNESS AROUND YORKVILLE MIDDLE SCHOOL?

Come paint a rock and add it to the Kindness Rock Garden in the courtyard! Right before Thanksgiving is the perfect time to realize how fortunate we all are, and show gratitude and spread kindness!

Any questions? Find Gabby Katz in the lobby before school all week to learn more!

YORKVILLE = KIND!

KINDNESS ROCKS!

From: Gabrielle Katz
To: Prianka Basak, Cecily Anderson
Subject: I'm sorry

Pri and Cece:

I don't feel like I fully apologized for the whole lunch table situation. I totally messed up. I did want to branch out and I still do and I'm so glad Miriam and the Hannahs are sitting with us, but I shouldn't have left you guys behind like that. It wasn't right. I know things are okay between us now but I am still really sorry.

Love you guys,
Gabs

Love

Peace

Hugs

Share smiles

Lend
a hand

Puppies &
rainbows

Always be
a friend

Thank
your
mom

You're never too old to cuddle

Find the sunshine

Beauty is all around us

Imagination is forever

KINDNESS ROCKS

Bravery & courage

GO FROM STRENGTH TO STRENGTH

KINDNESS DOES ROCK

CECILY

Gabs ur rock garden idea was soooooo fab

A million kids came out & it was freezing

GABRIELLE

IK

Soooooo excited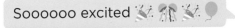

CECILY

This has been such a crazy start 2 the year

Can't believe it's already thanksgiving

GABRIELLE

IK

CECILY

Where r Pri & Vic ? ? ? 🧕 🧕

GABRIELLE

Prob @ swim LOL 🏊 🏊 🏊

CECILY

IK 😀 😀

Wahhhh sorry we r dropouts 🐱 😔 😢

GABRIELLE

Was Coach Sally B. Wembly mad 🤢 🤢 LOL

I never asked u

CECILY

She was glad I spoke 2 her in person 🗣 🗣

She understood the play took up a ton of time 🎭 🎭

Plus those 2 girls from the Jewish day school joined so that made up 4 us leaving 🧍 🧍 🧍

GABRIELLE

Oh

CECILY

Yeah it worked out

GABRIELLE

OMG when Pri & Vic get done w/ swim
they will have sooo many texts

CECILY

True

I gtg practice play lines

GABRIELLE

K love ya

CECILY

Mwah

Guyssssssssss

VICTORIA

Can u pls FaceTime me from the trip

So sad we can't go

PRIANKA

We will

CECILY

Promise

VICTORIA

Have so much fun

GABRIELLE

Wait guys

IDK if we can

My mom said no phones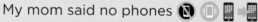

226

VICTORIA

Whatttttttttt 😲 😲 😲 😲

GABRIELLE

Yeah 😔 🙄 🙄

So sorry, Vic 😫 😫 😫

CECILY

We'll see what we can do 💪 💪

Finishing packing now 🎒 🎒

GABRIELLE

Luv u all 🤍 🤍 🤍 🤍

VICTORIA

Wahhhhhhhhh 😿 😿 😿 😿 😿 😿

THANKSGIVING
BORRRRRINNNGGGG

G   C   P   V

GABRIELLE

Hi guysssss

Totes texting u under the table

This is so boring

My uncle has been going on for a million minutes about how angry he is at the government

CECILY

Ha

Same here actually

PRIANKA

Hahaahahaahah

PRIANKA

My mom doesn't even really do
Thanksgiving food

But we all get 2gether anyway

VICTORIA

My cousins r here so it's fun

GABRIELLE

Nice

I have an idea

Let's text each other what we r thankful for

I'll go 1st

I'm thankful u guys forgave me

& still want to be my friends

CECILY

I'm thankful for my mom's sweet potatoes

U guys obvvvvvvv

PRIANKA

I'm thankful for my crazy wacky Indian fam

& poetry LOL

& u guys even tho ur
sometimes

VICTORIA

LOL LOL

I'm thankful u put up w me & all my mama
drama

GABRIELLE

K all of this

GABRIELLE

Getting glares now from peeps @ the table

Gtg

love you guys!!

CECILY

mwaaaahhhh

happy turkey

VICTORIA

yours forever in cranberry sauce 😂 🤣 😂

CECILY

ewwwww

VICTORIA

LOL

PRIANKA

k bye for real now

MILLCREEK
MOUNTAIN HOUSE

Guys our moms are totally making fun of us.
They brought their own shared notebook.
For real.

OMG they are so funny, and weird.

I'm glad we can at least write notes, though,
or they'd hear everything we were saying.

This place is so cool. I kinda wish we didn't
have to go to teen camp and could just
hang out.

That's what you say about literally everything, Pri.

MILLCREEK
MOUNTAIN HOUSE

LOL it's true. Ha whatever I'm proud of who I am. Seriously cannot believe Gabs was friends with Sami M. for five minutes this year. How weird???

She did become kind of nuts but Sami was fun at first. She has like tons of energy and is soooo outgoing but do you guys like Miriam?

She's okay. I like the Hannah from the play better.

Yeah she's nice.

Eloise and Sami sit alone @ their old table now?

MILLCREEK
MOUNTAIN HOUSE

Guess so. Guys want to go for a night swim after dinner? The indoor pool looks amaze.

Sure but why are we writing this? None of it is private. We can talk out loud LOL.

LOL but yeah isn't it fun to have a record of this? Have you guys gone back and read shared notebook lately? It's so funny. We need to keep this going until we go to college. k?

It is so funny, I agree.

Yes, I love it so much.

MILLCREEK
MOUNTAIN HOUSE

Okay so night swim and then can we stay up super late? So glad we have our own room. Also how amazing is the snow????

Yesssssssssssss soooooo pretty.

Same same sameeeeyyyyyy. Love this plan!

MILLCREEK
MOUNTAIN HOUSE

Okay now I do have something super secret to write since we are @ dinner and moms are talking nonstop... Cece, what do you think about having a party after the play? For cast and us and it could be super fun... sooo...thoughts? Is there already a cast party planned? Just realized there prob is.

Ummm, yes, there is! at my house! You guys come, too! It's just celebrating the cast but anyone can come.

Yess!!!!!!

MILLCREEK
MOUNTAIN HOUSE

We've never done a real party. Vishal had
that bday party and it was great except for
the Vic incident.

Hahaha that sounds like a TV show.

Totally does! But for real. A party would
be super fun. We need it after the drama
of this year so far. And before winter
break!!!!!

Ooh and Cece, your Christmas lights and tree
will be up and it will be soooooo pretty.

Yeahhhhhhh when are we coming over to
help decorate?

MILLCREEK
MOUNTAIN HOUSE

Next week?

Yay!

If it goes well, I think I want to do an end of year party in the backyard, too!!

YEAH! do both!

Guys do I look like a party animal?

Um no but you can become one!

Pos. Can we please leave this dinner? I'm telling the moms we can go back to the room and change into bathing suits and go for night swim on our own. There's a lifeguard there.

MILLCREEK
MOUNTAIN HOUSE

& Pri is still on the swim team. :)

Yessss I am a super professional swimmer.

← I'm doing it.

Dear Moms,

Thank you so much for this truly meaningful experience. We were really able to reconnect and remember how special our friendships are.

We are so lucky you met in that pregnant moms' group or whatever it was called. Sorry I can't remember! Not many people can say they've been friends since before they were even born.

This trip was so amazing! My favorite part was all the late night swims. Prettiest indoor pool I've ever seen. I also loved the food and the tea and cookies and the s'mores. That fire pit kept us so warm even though it's freezing here.

I loved the snowy hike we all took together and the view from the top of the mountain. I also loved sitting by the fireplace in the lobby.

I loved the creaky floors and the spooky, kind of haunted vibe of this place. I loved when we were all cozy in our matching pj's in the suite. It was all so perfect.

Thank you from the bottoms of our hearts.

Can this be an annual thing? :)

We love you!
Gabby, Prianka, and Cecily
♡ xoxo

GLOSSARY

2 to

2gether together

2morrow tomorrow

4 for

4eva forever

4get forget

any1 anyone

awk awkward

bc because

BFF best friends forever

BFFAE best friends forever and ever

BI Block Island

BNF best neighbors forever

b-room bathroom

b/t between

c see

caf cafeteria

comm committee

COMO crying over missing out

comp computer

deets details

def definitely

DEK don't even know

diff different

disc discussion

emo emotional

every1 everyone

fab fabulous

fabolicious extra fabulous

fac faculty

fave favorite

Fla Florida

FOMO fear of missing out

fone phone

FYI for your information

gd god

gg gotta go

Gma grandma

gn good night

gnight good night

gr8 great

gtg gotta go

hw homework

ICB I can't believe

IDC I don't care

IDEK I don't even know

IDK I don't know

IHNC I have no clue

IK I know

IKWYM I know what you mean

ILY I love you

ILYSM I love you so much

JK just kidding

K OK

KIA know-it-all

KWIM know what I mean

L8r later

LMK let me know

lol laugh out loud

luv love

n e way anyway

NM nothing much

nums numbers

nvm never mind

obv obviously

obvi obviously

obvs obviously

OMG oh my God

ooc out of control

PBFF poetry best friend forever

peeps people

perf perfect

pgs pages

plzzzz please

pos possibly

q question

r are / our

ridic ridiculous

rlly really

RN right now

sci science

sec second

sem semester

scheds schedules

shud should

some1 someone

SWAK sealed with a kiss

TBH to be honest

thx thanks

tm tomorrow

TMI too much information

tmrw tomorrow

tomrw tomorrow

tomw tomorrow

totes totally

ttyl talk to you later

u you

ur your

urself yourself

vv very, very

w/ with

wb write back

whatev whatever

WIGO what is going on

wknd weekend

w/o without

WTH what the heck

wud would

wut what

wuzzzz what's

Y why

ACKNOWLEDGMENTS

Oodles of thanks to the Katherine Tegen Books crew: Maria, Stephanie, Katherine, Kristen, Liz, Mark, Molly, Amy, and Vaishali; the BWL Library & Tech team; Alyssa and Alice at Trident; all the Greenwalds; all the Rosenbergs; and last but def not least each and every TBH reader. I luv u all. xoxoxoxoxoxoxox

Photo by Peter Dressel

LISA GREENWALD lives in NYC 🍎 w/ her husband & 2 young daughters 👨 👩 👧 👧. She 💙s: 😎 📚 🏖️ & 🍰. Summer is her favorite season ☀️ 🌞 🍉 🍨 🍦 🎆 🕶️. Visit her 💻 @ www.lisagreenwald.com.

Great books by
LISA GREENWALD!

The Friendship List

TBH

KT KATHERINE TEGEN BOOKS
An Imprint of HarperCollins Publishers

www.harpercollinschildrens.com